A Christmas Journey

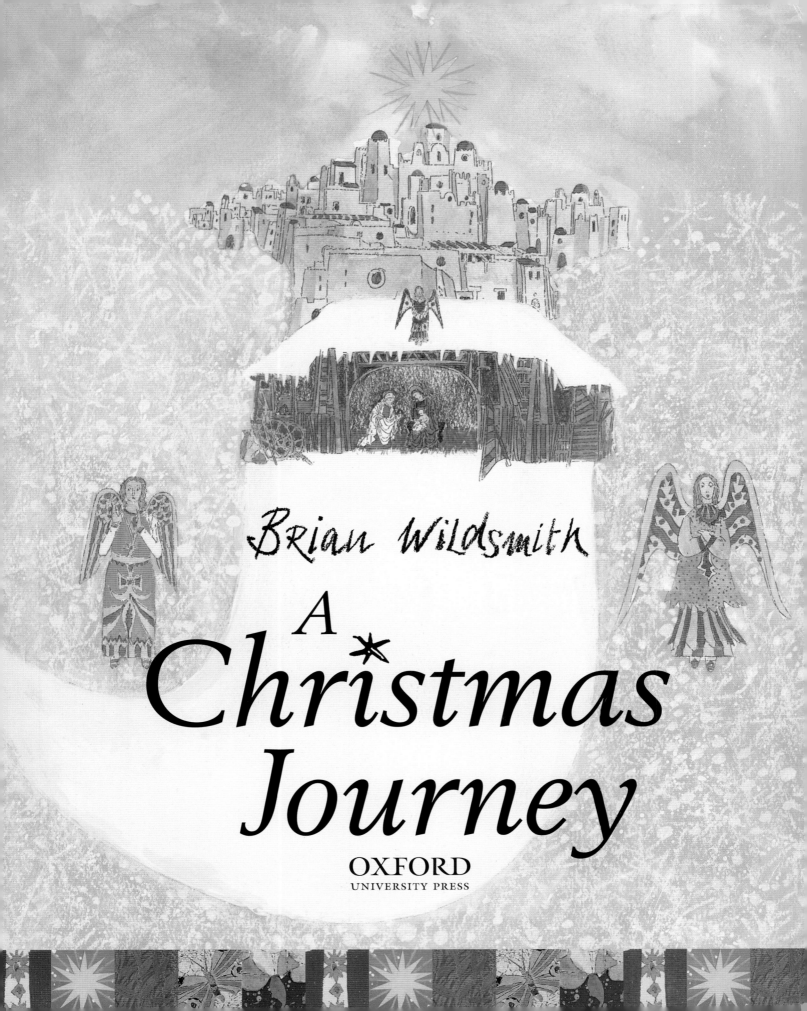

Brian Wildsmith

A
Christmas
Journey

OXFORD
UNIVERSITY PRESS

It was spring, and God sent the angel Gabriel to Nazareth to visit a young girl called Mary.
'You will have a son,' he said. 'His name will be Jesus and he will be called the Son of God.'

Some time later, Mary and her husband Joseph had to go to Bethlehem. As it was a long way, Mary could not take her cat and dog with her, so she left them with a neighbour to look after.

The cat and the dog missed Mary very much.
So one day they ran away to try and find her.

On their way they met a fox. He was stuck fast in a rabbit hole. Cat and Dog wanted to help him, so they pulled and pulled until Fox was free.

'Oh, thank you,' said Fox. 'Where are you going to?'

'To Bethlehem to find Mary.'

'Can I come too?'

'Yes, just follow us,' they replied. And off they went.

On their way they met a goat. He had got stuck in a cart while trying to steal some carrots. Cat, Dog, and Fox all wanted to help him, so they pulled and pulled until Goat was free.

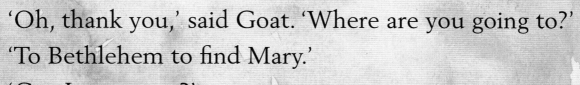

'Oh, thank you,' said Goat. 'Where are you going to?'
'To Bethlehem to find Mary.'
'Can I come too?'
'Yes, just follow us,' they replied. And off they went.

On their way they met a bear.
He had been caught in a hunter's trap
while trying to steal honey from a bees' nest.
Cat, Dog, Fox, and Goat all wanted to help him,
so they pulled and pulled until Bear was free.
'Oh, thank you,' said Bear. 'Where are you going to?'
'To Bethlehem to find Mary.'
'Can I come too?'
'Yes, just follow us,' they replied. And off they went.

They came to a big palace and there they met three camels.
'Where are you going to?' said the camels.
'To Bethlehem to find Mary.'

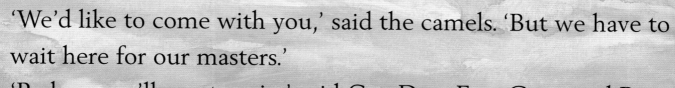

'We'd like to come with you,' said the camels. 'But we have to wait here for our masters.'

'Perhaps we'll meet again,' said Cat, Dog, Fox, Goat, and Bear. 'Goodbye.'

As they came near to Bethlehem, they met some sheep, grazing in a field.

'Where are you going to?' said the sheep.

'To Bethlehem to find Mary.'

'So are we. We know the way. Just follow us.'

When they reached Bethlehem, they could not see Mary in the inn. Instead they found her in the stable with her new-born baby.

Mary was delighted to see Cat and Dog and their friends.
'Come in,' she said, 'and meet my baby. His name is Jesus.'

Then the three camels arrived, carrying three kings.
'We have followed a shining star,' said the kings.
And kneeling down, they offered the baby their
gifts of gold, frankincense, and myrrh.

'Our journey is ended now,' said Cat and Dog. 'We have
found Mary and her baby Jesus, who is the Son of God.'

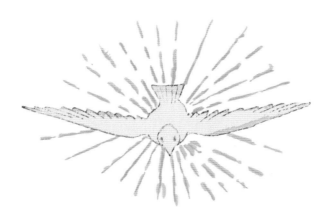

For all children, young and old.

OXFORD
UNIVERSITY PRESS

Great Clarendon Street, Oxford OX2 6DP

Oxford University Press is a department of the University of Oxford.
It furthers the University's objective of excellence in research, scholarship,
and education by publishing worldwide in

Oxford   New York

Auckland   Cape Town   Dar es Salaam   Hong Kong   Karachi
Kuala Lumpur   Madrid   Melbourne   Mexico City   Nairobi
New Delhi   Shanghai   Taipei   Toronto

With offices in

Argentina   Austria   Brazil   Chile   Czech Republic   France   Greece
Guatemala   Hungary   Italy   Japan   Poland   Portugal   Singapore
South Korea   Switzerland   Thailand   Turkey   Ukraine   Vietnam

Oxford is a registered trade mark of Oxford University Press
in the UK and in certain other countries

First published in 2003 as *The Road to Bethlehem*
This edition first published in 2010

Text and illustrations © Brian Wildsmith 2003, 2010

British Library Cataloguing in Publication Data available

ISBN: 978-0-19-278980-8 (paperback)

2 4 6 8 10 9 7 5 3 1

Printed in China

Paper used in the production of this book is a natural,
recyclable product made from wood grown in sustainable forests.
The manufacturing process conforms to the environmental
regulations of the country of origin